For Collin
& Riley
Go Green

Colonel Trash Truck

by Kathleen Crawley

Keeping The Planet Clean and Green

illustrations by Manuel Conde

Publishers Cataloging-in-Publication Data

Crawley, Kathleen.
   Colonel Trash Truck : keeping the planet clean and green /
by Kathleen Crawley ; illustrations by Manuel Conde.
      p. cm.
   (Colonel Trash Truck and his clean and green team)
   Summary: Describes how Colonel Trash Truck and his army
of trash trucks collect the trash and keep the town clean and green.
   ISBN-13: 978-1-60131-033-0
   [1. Refuse collection vehicles—Juvenile fiction. 2. Refuse
and refuse disposal—Juvenile fiction. 3. Trucks—Juvenile
fiction. 4. Recycling (Waste, etc.)—Juvenile fiction.]
   I. Conde, Manuel, ill. II. Title.
                                    2008929007

115 Bluebill Drive
Savannah, GA 31419
United States
(888) 300-1961

To order additional copies please go to www.ColonelTrashTruck.com

This book was published with the assistance of the helpful folks at DragonPencil.com

For my sister, Mary Cooper – thank you for inspiring me to write Colonel Trash Truck. No one makes me laugh harder.

And for my husband, Ronald Thomson – I thank God every day for your unconditional love and support. You are my hero.

Kathy

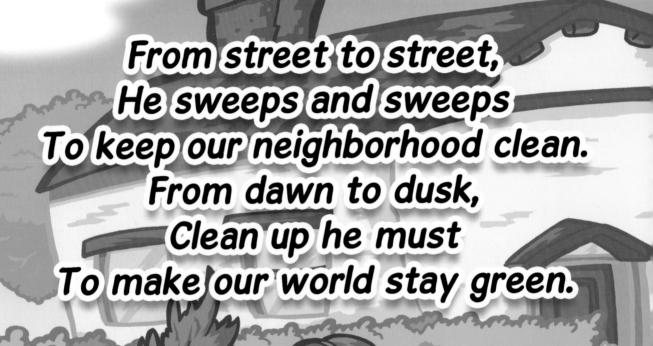

From street to street,
He sweeps and sweeps
To keep our neighborhood clean.
From dawn to dusk,
Clean up he must
To make our world stay green.

His arms are strong,
Work all day long
And fill his bins with clutter,
Go up and down
And all around town.
Oh, how the litterbugs shudder!

He is not small,
But wide and tall,
And keeps the scum away.
He picks up waste
And, in much haste,
He keeps all filth at bay.

He chomps on trash,
Even corned beef hash;
He eats garbage for lunch.
He grinds it down
And makes the sound:
"Karunch, Karunch, Karunch!"

He picks up leaves
That fall from trees
Or are blown down by the wind.
Used plates and cups—
He picks them up,
So litterbugs never win.

There's gunk and grime
And stuff with slime
That he gets out of sight
And wrappers and lids
Left by many kids.
He cleans with all his might.

He leads the charge
Of armies large
That fight the garbage war.
His troops salute,
Are resolute,
To make roads shine once more.

His soldiers are true,
Removing doo doo
Of cats and dogs and others.
They'll even come
Pick up the scum
Left by your little brother.

THE CLEAN AND GREEN TEAM

They'll never give up,
Sundown or sunup,
To clean, no matter the mess.
United they stand
At the Colonel's command,
But it's you who they want to impress.

And don't forget
To never let
Your paper and bottles be mixed.
Save our trees;
Recycle please,
Especially when it's plastic.

The beverage you drink,
Whether orange or pink,
That comes in a bright shiny can,
Should be put in the bin
For the Colonel to bring in
And be "karunched" down and used once again.

He wants you to know
You must always say, "No!"
When told that it just doesn't matter.
Recycling is key
And always will be.
Yes, ignore all that negative chatter!

The Colonel will never
Consider surrender
To those who would want to destroy
Our beautiful land,
The dirt or the sand,
And parks that we like to enjoy.

Please give him a hand,
And do understand
That he wants to keep the world clean.
He does it for us,
No matter the fuss,
And hopes that we try to live green.

So next time you hear
The crunch and the gears
Of the trash truck 'round the bend,
Be of good cheer
And do not fear.
Colonel Trash Truck is your friend!

ABOUT THE AUTHOR

Kathleen Crawley has been an advertising executive for over fifteen years. She resides with her husband Ronal[d] Thomson in Redondo Beach, California. She is a native Californian, having graduated from UCLA with a B.A. i[n] Sociology. Colonel Trash Truck is her first book. About writing for children, Kathy says, "I have a number of book[s] that I want to write for kids because I think children are fascinating. They are open, creative, and interested i[n] everything; they bring out the kid in me!"

ABOUT THE ILLUSTRATOR

Manuel "MACS" Conde has been in the comics and fantasy industry for nineteen amazing years. He and his wif[e] and their young child spend half the year south of the border, and the other half in sunny San Diego, CA. He love[s] creating bold, vibrant illustrations, especially for younger children. "Remember when you were a little kid[?] Well, don't you dare forget it!"

THIS BOOK HAS BEEN PRINTED USING
THE HIGHEST POSSIBLE PERCENTAGE
OF POST-CONSUMER WASTE THAT
CURRENT TECHNOLOGY ALLOWS.